THE
SESAME STREET
BOOK OF

FAIRY TALES

FEATURING
JIM HENSON'S
MUPPETS

By
Emily Perl Kingsley
David Korr   Jeffrey Moss

Illustrated by
Joseph Mathieu

Random House/Children's Television Workshop

Copyright © 1975 Children's Television Workshop. MUPPET Characters © 1971, 1972, 1973, 1975 Muppets, Inc. "Sesame Street" and the "Sesame Street" sign are trademarks and servicemarks of Children's Television Workshop. All rights reserved under International and Pan-American Copyright Conventions. Published in the United States by Random House, Inc., New York, and simultaneously in Canada by Random House of Canada Limited, Toronto. Library of Congress Cataloging in Publication Data: Kingsley, Emily Perl. The Sesame Street book of fairy tales. Characters from the series produced by the Children's Television Workshop. SUMMARY: Three fairy tales featuring the Muppets relate the adventures of Lord Ludwig of Liverwurst, King Marvin the Magnificent, and the King of Cauliflower. [1. Fairy tales] I. Korr, David, joint author. II. Moss, Jeffrey, joint author. III. Mathieu, Joseph. IV. Children's Television Workshop. V. Sesame Street. VI. Title. PZ8.K6193Se [E] 75-1606 ISBN 0-394-83131-4 ISBN 0-394-93131-9 lib. bdg. Manufactured in the United States of America.
1   2   3   4   5   6   7   8   9   0.

CONTENTS

5

6

7

The King of Cauliflower's Castle

Once upon a time, in the Kingdom of Cauliflower, there was a King. The King lived in a very nice castle. But the King was not satisfied.

I'm not satisfied. This castle isn't big enough. I want a bigger castle. I want it big, BIG, BIG. Call the Royal Carpenter.

Royal Carpenter!

Royal Carpenter!

I wonder what he wants now— wheels for his throne, or something?

Soon, the royal workpeople were hard at work, building the King a bigger castle.

And the castle grew and grew . . .

. . . and grew, until it went right up to the edge of the
Kingdom of Cauliflower in every direction. In the
North, it touched the fence between Cauliflower and
the land of Rutabaga. In the South, it bumped right
into the United States of Spinach. In the West, it cast
its shadow on the good people of Broccoli. And in the
East, it looked right down on the hills and valleys
of Canteloupe.

11

But the castle was *so* big, there was no room *outside* in the land of Cauliflower. The whole land of Cauliflower was *inside* the castle. And that caused problems. The King's cows couldn't find any grass to eat. . . .

And His Highness's hens and the royal rooster couldn't find any bugs or seeds to eat.

And His Highness's horse had no place to run around.

So what do you think happened next?

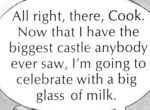

All right, there, Cook. Now that I have the biggest castle anybody ever saw, I'm going to celebrate with a big glass of milk.

There's no more milk, Your Majesty. The cows couldn't find any grass to eat, so they all went to work in the Kingdom of Rutabaga.

Oh, yeah? Well, then fry me an egg.

But there was no place for the hens to lay any eggs, Your Majesty, so they all went to work in the United States of Spinach.

This is terrible! Groom, saddle my horse and I will ride after them.

The horse went to Broccoli, Your Majesty. He said there was no place for him to run around here.

Oh, boy! Well, I guess I'll take a bath. The bathtub didn't leave, did it?

QUACK QUACK QUACK

But, oh dear, His Majesty's mackerels and the Queen's quackers were in the bathtub, because there weren't any more lakes and rivers in Cauliflower. And even worse...

14

...all the Royal Staircases were covered with flower pots.

So the King ordered the Carpenter to make the castle smaller. Then there would be room outside for Princess Peony's flowers, and the cows and the hens and the horse would come back. "And then," yelled the King, "you can get the fish out of my bathtub!"

And so, the royal workpeople took the big new castle apart and put back the old small one. And sure enough, the cows came back, and the chickens came back, and the horse came back . . .

But the King of Cauliflower had learned a very important lesson—BIGGER is not always BETTER.

19

King Marvin the Magnificent was very grand indeed.
He said, "I am magnificent." His subjects all agreed.
"King Marvin is magnificent! Our kingdom is most blest.
Of all the Kings who ever were, King Marvin is the best."

Now in King Marvin's kingdom lived a little boy named Paul
Whose favorite thing was playing with a bright pink rubber ball.
He bounced his rubber ball all day against the palace gate.
He started in the morning and he stayed till it grew late.

One day as he was playing ball, he stopped and said, "I know!
I think I'll throw my rubber ball as high as it will go."
So Paul wound up and threw the ball with one tremendous fling.
"Oh, no!" he cried. "It's headed for the window of the King!"

Smash! went the royal window,
and before the King could duck,
The ball bounced off
King Marvin's throne . . .

and hit his nose . . .

and stuck.

"What *is* this thing?" said Marvin
    as he felt the ball and sneered.
But before he could remove it,
    his Prime Minister appeared.

"King Marv!" cried the Prime Minister.
    "A rubber ball! How cute!
    It really is magnificent! I'll get one for *my* snoot."

And like a flash he left the room, and what do you suppose?
When he returned, a rubber ball was stuck upon *his* nose.

23

The news spread quickly through the land
(the kingdom was quite small).
Soon on each person's nose there was
a bright pink rubber ball.

The butcher and the baker and the driver of the bus
All said, "If Marvin likes it, then it's good enough for us."

"Don't we look great!" the people cried.
     "Our noses are so pleasing!
Except it's rather hard to smell, and even harder sneezing."

But everyone was happy, the whole kingdom filled with joy,
For everybody had a ball—except for one small boy.

"Oh, woe," cried Paul, "without my ball
I really am so sad.
I'll ask the King to give it back—
I hope he won't be mad."

Paul tiptoed to the throne room
    where King Marvin was alone.
The King in his magnificence
    sat on his royal throne.

Young Paul knelt down before the King
    and then was told to rise,
But when he lifted up his head
    a strange sight met his eyes.
King Marvin wore an ermine cloak,
    silk slippers on his toes,
A golden crown was on his head . . .
    and a ball was on his nose.

Then Paul began to giggle, and he laughed till he was sore,
And pretty soon he laughed so hard, he fell down on the floor.

"What's so funny?" said King Marvin,
    as he saw that Paul was staring.
"It's your nose!" cried Paul with laughter.
    "That's my favorite toy you're wearing."

    "My nose looks great!" King Marvin said.
    Said Paul, "I beg to differ.
    You really do look silly
    with that ball stuck on your sniffer."

    "I do?" exclaimed King Marvin.
    "Bring my royal mirror quick."
    King Marvin looked. He saw himself,
    and what he said was…"Ick!"

    "I really do look silly,
    and I knew it from the first.
    I've always said that rubber balls
    on noses are the worst!"

The King took off the rubber ball and handed it to Paul.
"You've taught me a great lesson,
    so I'll give you back your ball."
Then the butcher and the baker and the driver of the bus
Said, "If Marvin gave his ball away...
                    that's good enough for us!"

The people of the kingdom gave their rubber balls away
And they all have worn their noses plain...
                    ... right to this very day.

So from early in the morning time until it grows quite late,
Paul has a hundred balls to bounce against the palace gate.

Now this story has a moral
And it's very, very true—
If a king does something silly
You don't have to do it too.

Long, long ago, in a lavish lodge near the village of
Liverwurst, lived a lovely lass called Linda the Lonely.
Linda was lonely because, ever since she was a little
girl, she had been locked in the lodge by her wicked
uncle, Lord Ludwig of Liverwurst.

"Alas, alack. What a lousy life I live!" lamented Linda.
"Let me loose! Let me loose!"

But Lord Ludwig laughed loudly. "Not likely, my little
lamb! I still have loads and loads of work for you to do!"

For long hours Linda labored in Lord Ludwig's library, lifting lots and lots of books. Every day Lord Ludwig would yell, "Linda, you lunk, stop loafing! Where is my lunch? It is late."

Linda lugged Lord Ludwig's large lunch from the larder.

"What have you brought me, you little lump?" asked Lord Ludwig as Linda ladled out his luscious lunch of leafy lettuce, large lobsters, lovely lentils, lima beans, leg of lamb, licorice, lollipops and lemonade.

"Oh, Uncle Ludwig!" Linda lamented, "I have been laboring long hours on your library ladder! Please let me have a little lunch, too."

"Later, lazybones... if there's any lunch left! Ha, ha! Now leave— and get back to your ladder!"

Late one night, in the loft where she lived, Linda laid her lonely head upon her lumpy little bed. Suddenly she heard voices. Linda leaned out the window to listen.

Lord Ludwig and a lanky lad were on the lawn. "I know I am late with your laundry, Lord Ludwig," said the lad. "But there is so little light and it is such a *large* load of laundry."

"None of your lip, lout! Get a lamp if there is no light—but lather up that laundry or there will be lots of lashes where you least like 'em!"

With that, Lord Ludwig left.

33

Linda took a lantern and leaned out of the window. She leapt onto the limb of a lemon tree, and lowered herself lightly onto the lawn.

"Who are you?" asked the lanky lad.

"I am Lord Ludwig's niece, Linda the Lonely. Who are you?"

"I am Lloyd of London, Lord Ludwig's lowliest lackey. And I am lonely, too."

"Listen, Lloyd," lilted Linda. "I have long longed to leave this loathsome lodge. Let me tell you my plan! Listen..."

"La," laughed Lloyd. "It's so loony, it just might work!"

Late the next day, Lloyd lugged his load of laundry into Lord Ludwig's library. "Look, Linda," said Lloyd as he lifted his lute from under Ludwig's lavender leggings. "I have brought my lute."

"It's lovely, Lloyd. Now lend me your long leather laces so I can make a lasso."

Linda told Lloyd
to lull Lord Ludwig
with a lilting
lullaby on his lute.
Soon Lord Ludwig
was fast asleep.

Like lightning, Linda looped her lasso around Lord Ludwig's legs and lashed him to the library ladder.

"Help!" yelled Lord Ludwig. "I want to call my lawyer."

"You'll have lots of time for that, you lily-livered lizard! You're going to learn your lesson. You'll be locked up for a long, long time, laboring in the laundry of the local jail!"

Linda lifted a large key from Ludwig's leather belt, unlocked the lodge's locks and lifted the latch.

"Now, Lloyd, let's leave!" laughed Linda.

"Linda," said Lloyd, "it was a lucky day for me when you leapt from that lemon tree."

"Then we shall call you Lloyd the Lucky," said Linda.

"And you shall be Linda the Lionhearted," said Lloyd.

"And," they said together, "we won't be lonely any longer."

I have finally found a story that has no pigs, no bears, no kittens—no nothing. This is the story of <u>Snow White</u>.

Sounds good to me. Snow White... seems to me I've heard that story before...oh, well, go on.

You mean you don't want to stop me to count anything?

Nope. Just one girl, Snow White. Not much to count there. One girl. But I do seem to remember something wonderful about this story.... Go ahead.